GHOUL DINNERS

St Sebastian's new dinner lady, Miss Grub, was hunched over a huge metal vat of green gruel. She was muttering phrases and stopping, then starting again. She scratched her head and huge flakes of dandruff drifted into her cooking.

The caretaker, Mr Wharpley, decided to have a taste. *It looks a bit thin, but I know women love it when you flatter their cooking,* he thought to himself.

James, Lenny and Alexander saw what was about to happen. As the man raised a spoonful of bewitched soup to his lips, the boys sprang from under the table and charged towards him. James ran the fastest, with his arms outstretched, ready to knock the spoon out of Mr Wharpley's hand.

'Noooooo!' he roared. But it was too late. Mr Wharpley had already pushed the spoon of soup into his mouth, and had swallowed.

St Sebastian's School in Grimesford is the pits. No, really — it is.

Every year, the high school sinks a bit further into the boggy plague pit beneath it and, every year, the ghosts of the plague victims buried underneath it become a bit more cranky.

Egged on by their spooky ringleader, Edith Codd, they decide to get their own back — and they're willing to play dirty. *Really* dirty.

They kick up a stink by causing as much mischief as in inhumanly possible so as to get St Sebastian's closed down once and for all.

But what they haven't reckoned on is year-seven new boy, James Simpson and his friends Alexander and Lenny.

The question is, are the gang up to the challenge of laying St Sebastian's paranormal problem to rest, or will their school remain forever frightful?

There's only one way to find out . . .

www.too-ghoul.com

TOO GHOUL FOR SCHOOL

Ghoul Dinners

B. STRANGE

EGMONT

Special thanks to:

Lynn Huggins-Cooper, St John's Walworth Church of England Primary School and Belmont Primary School

EGMONT
We bring stories to life

Published in Great Britain 2007
by Egmont UK Limited
239 Kensington High Street, London W8 6SA

Text & illustrations © 2007 Egmont UK Ltd
Text by Lynn Huggins-Cooper
Illustrations by Pulsar Studio (Beehive Illustration)

ISBN 978 1 4052 3238 8

1 3 5 7 9 10 8 6 4 2

A CIP catalogue record for this title is available
from the British Library

Typeset by Avon DataSet Ltd, Bidford on Avon, Warwickshire
Printed and bound in Great Britain by the CPI Group

'More books – I love it!'
Ashley, age 11

'It's disgusting. . .'
Joe, age 10

'. . . it's all good!'
Alexander, age 9

'. . . loads of excitement and really gross!'
Jay, age 9

'I like the way there's the brainy boy,
the brawny boy and the cool boy that form a
team of friends'
Charlie, age 10

'That ghost Edith is wicked'
Matthew, age 11

'This is really good and funny!'
Sam, age 9

School versus . . .

Year-seven new boy and chief spook-hunter

James Simpson

Headmaster's son and official brainiac

Alexander Tick

Strong as an ox, gentle as an unusually tall lamb

Lenny Maxwell

...Ghoul!

Loud-mouthed ringleader of the plague-pit ghosts

Edith Codd

Young ghost and a secret wannabe St Sebastian's pupil

William Scroggins

Bone idle ex-leech merchant with a taste for all things gross

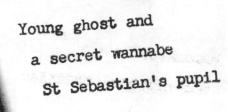

Ambrose Harbottle

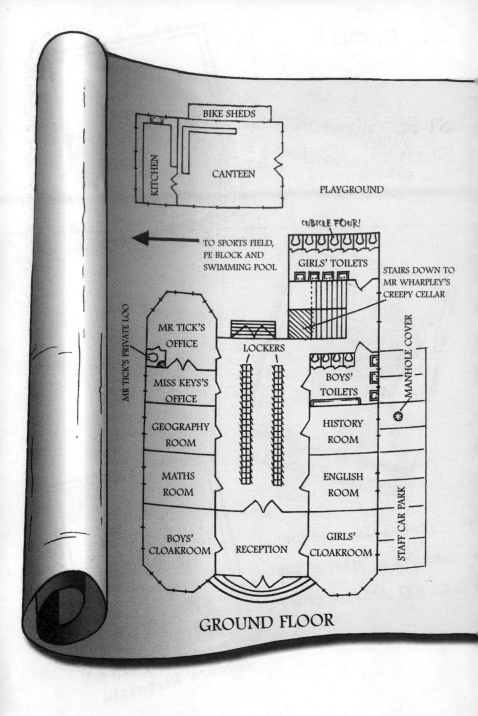

BIKE SHEDS

KITCHEN

CANTEEN

PLAYGROUND

CUBICLE FOUR!

TO SPORTS FIELD,
PE BLOCK AND
SWIMMING POOL

GIRLS' TOILETS

STAIRS DOWN TO
MR WHARPLEY'S
CREEPY CELLAR

MR TICK'S PRIVATE LOO

MR TICK'S
OFFICE

LOCKERS

MISS KEYS'S
OFFICE

BOYS'
TOILETS

MANHOLE COVER

GEOGRAPHY
ROOM

HISTORY
ROOM

MATHS
ROOM

ENGLISH
ROOM

STAFF CAR PARK

BOYS'
CLOAKROOM

RECEPTION

GIRLS'
CLOAKROOM

GROUND FLOOR

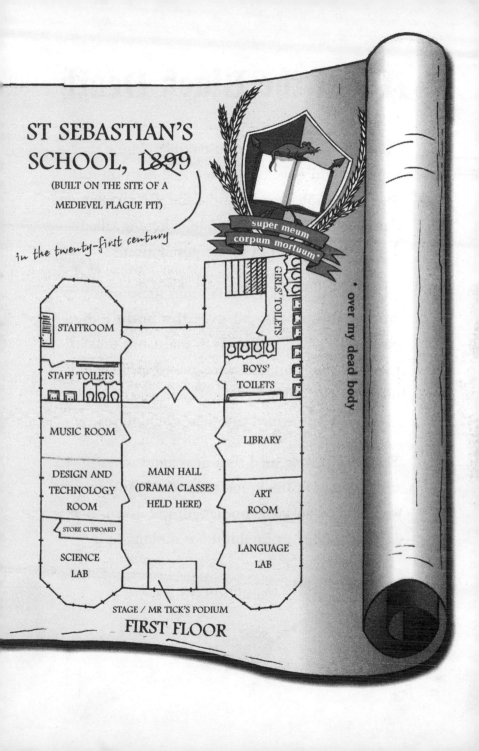

About the Black Death

The Black Death was a terrible plague that
is believed to have been spread by fleas on rats.
It swept through Europe in the fourteenth century,
arriving in England in 1348, where it killed
over one third of the population.

One of the Black Death's main symptoms was
**foul-smelling boils all over the body called
'buboes'**. The plague was so infectious that its
victims and their families were locked in their houses
until they died. Many villages were abandoned as
the disease wiped out their populations.

So many people died that graveyards overflowed
and bodies lay in the street, so special **'plague pits'**
were dug to bury the bodies. Almost every town
and village in England has a plague pit
somewhere underneath it, so watch out
when you're digging in the garden . . .

Dear Reader

As you may have already guessed, B. Strange is not a real name.

The author of this series is an ex-teacher who is currently employed by a little-known body called the Organisation For Spook Termination (Excluding Demons), or O.F.S.T.(E.D.). 'B. Strange' is the pen name chosen to protect his identity.

Together, we felt it was our duty to publish these books, in an attempt to save innocent lives. The stories are based on the author's experiences as an O.F.S.T.(E.D.) inspector in various schools over the past two decades.

Please read them carefully - you may regret it if you don't . . .

Yours sincerely
The Publisher.

PS - Should you wish to file a report on any suspicious supernatural occurrences at your school, visit **www.too-ghoul.com** and fill out the relevant form. We'll pass it on to O.F.S.T.(E.D.) for you.

PPS - All characters' names have been changed to protect the identity of the individuals. Any similarity to actual persons, living or undead, is purely coincidental.

CONTENTS

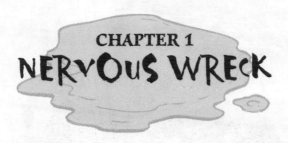

CHAPTER 1
NERVOUS WRECK

Mrs Cooper, St Sebastian's longest-serving dinner lady, was singing happily to a song on the radio. A huge vat of bolognese sauce bubbled on the cooker top, and the kitchen was filled with the rich smell of tomatoes. She danced across to the huge fridge, her bottom swaying as she moved in time to the music, shaking a jar of oil in one hand like a maraca.

'Cheese . . . that's what I need . . .' Mrs Cooper sang, as she grabbed the door handle. The door swung open and icy vapour curled out of the

fridge. 'Funny . . . I must have the setting too cold . . .' she muttered to herself, pulling the door open wide.

She shrieked as she came face to face with a severed head, sitting on the top shelf. It dripped blood on to the shelves below. The head blew her a kiss, and winked.

'Hello, darling!' a raspy male voice laughed.

Mrs Cooper dropped the jar of oil and it shattered on the floor with a crash. Mrs Meadows, her fellow dinner lady, rushed into the kitchen carrying a huge bag of frozen chips.

'What's the matter, love? Did you cut yourself?' She rushed over to Mrs Cooper's side. 'I heard you scream . . .'

'It's . . . it's . . .' Mrs Cooper pointed at the fridge with a shaking finger. Mrs Meadows nudged her out of the way.

'Can't see anything that bad, Lynn. There's a mouldy-looking piece of cheddar but we can cut the edges off . . .' she rummaged further.

'But there's a – a head!'

'Of slimy lettuce. Yes, I know – if the headmaster sees it we'll get another lecture about "the importance of running a tight ship", but it's not *that* bad. Here! I'll stash it in the bins.'

She bustled past Mrs Cooper who was still staring at the fridge, wide-eyed. 'You have a sit-down, love,' Mrs Meadows frowned. 'I'll pop the kettle on for a brew – that'll make you feel better!'

Mrs Cooper sat down heavily. Her eyes kept darting back to the fridge. The kettle started to boil with a loud whistle and she jumped out of her seat.

'You are jittery this morning, Lynn! What's wrong?' Mrs Meadows asked, turning off the kettle and putting her arm around her friend.

'N-n-nothing, Sue!' Mrs Cooper smiled, bravely. 'Just my imagination playing tricks again.' She shook her head and her perm bobbed up and down. 'Our Alex had us all awake late last night playing his flaming rock music. I'm just tired, that's all!' she laughed shakily and got up.

'Oh – don't get me started on teenagers! Our Joanne has me in a flap most days. Kids! Come on – I'll make that tea. Then we'd better get the fryer going for these chips.'

Mrs Cooper looked over her shoulder towards the fridge and shuddered, then she turned on the tap to fill a huge pan with water for the spaghetti.

Deep in the store cupboard, something was stirring. A mouse nibbled at the corner of a packet of raisins and squeaked with excitement as the brown treasures tumbled out of the hole. It didn't notice the green, glowing mist that slid along the shelf behind it. The mouse stuffed its cheeks happily with sweet treats.

The mist rose until it towered over the creature. It started to take on a shape: first a fat, furry body and then a long, fluffy tail, next came four paws with long, razor-sharp claws and, finally, a face topped by pointed ears and a mouthful of teeth like daggers.

The mouse stopped eating. Its whiskers twitched and it cocked its head on one side to listen. A strange, rumbling sound filled the store cupboard. It had heard that noise before – it was the sound of a cat purring!

The mouse spun round to see green eyes glittering in the darkness. A huge paw shot out and stamped on its tail. The mouse was trapped. It pulled and squeaked, its heart beating fast. It gave an almighty heave, and its tail stretched thin.

At that moment, the cat lifted a paw and the mouse shot away across the cupboard, hitting packets as it fell, like a furry ball in a pinball machine. The cat seemed to smile, and then started to dissolve back into mist. It liked torturing small, defenceless things. And dinner ladies.

Back in the kitchen, Mrs Cooper was whisking a bowl of chocolate mousse. After her cup of tea, she felt much better. She poured the sticky mixture into lines of plastic pots. Putting the bowl in the dishwasher, she opened the store-cupboard door.

'Hmmm, where did I put those pots of sprinkles . . .? Oh – these will do!' she grabbed a large plastic tub of jelly drops. 'I hope there's enough left . . .' she raised the tub to look and screamed. It was a jar of eyeballs!

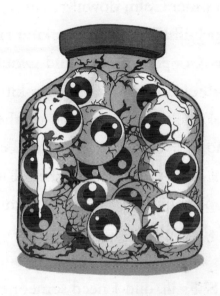

Mrs Cooper dropped the tub and ran backwards and forwards in the cupboard in blind panic. She knocked bottles and jars off shelves and as she fell back on to a tall, wobbly set of shelves, a bag of flour toppled over and covered her in a white cloud.

Mrs Meadows came barrelling in to the cupboard and grabbed Mrs Cooper, who screamed even louder.

'Lynn! It's me! Calm down!'

'Eyes! Eyeballs! They were looking right at me . . .' Mrs Cooper groaned and swayed. Mrs Meadows steered her back into the kitchen.

'Sit there!' she ordered, picking up the phone and ringing Mr Wharpley, the school caretaker.

'Reg? It's Sue here, in the kitchen. I need your help. No, nothing's broken – well, nothing I can't deal with,' she sighed, looking at the broken jars and bottles on the floor of the store cupboard. 'It's Lynn. She's ill, and I need someone to drive her home. Thanks, Reg. Yes, I owe you a chocolate fudge cake for this!' she smiled.

She put the phone down and bobbed down next to her friend. 'I think you need a rest, love.

Reg is going to take you home, and I'll ring your Kev at work to let him know you're poorly.'

Mrs Cooper stared past Mrs Meadows, chewing her lip. 'Eyeballs . . .' she whispered.

Moments later, Mr Wharpley and Mrs Meadows steered the shaking dinner lady into Mr Wharpley's van.

As it pulled away from the kerb noisily, Mrs Meadows sighed. 'Poor Lynn!' She shook her head. 'And poor me!' she groaned.

Then she trudged back to the kitchen to prepare three hundred portions of chips by herself.

The next day, the headmaster, Mr Tick, was humming to himself as he played solitaire on the computer in his office. A cup of coffee steamed on his desk, and Miss Keys had left a plate of his favourite crumble creams within easy reach. All was well with the world.

Mr Tick looked up, thinking hard about his next move, when he saw a shadow through the frosted glass in his office door. He sighed and his shoulders sagged. He opened the Department for Education web page to hide his game of solitaire and called, 'Enter!'

His secretary, Miss Keys, scuttled in, biting her lip nervously.

'Well? What is it? Something important to justify disturbing my work, I presume . . .?' Mr Tick growled.

'Erm, I'm afraid Lynn Cooper has just rung to say she won't be in today and won't be back in the foreseeable future. Well, it was her husband, actually. He said she was very poorly and couldn't come to the phone. The doctor has signed her off work with her nerves.'

'Well, he couldn't sign her off without her nerves, could he?' chuckled Mr Tick at his own joke.

Miss Keys looked puzzled.

Mr Tick sighed. 'I don't know why I bother . . .' he grumbled under his breath and frowned. 'Lynn Cooper? I don't remember any teachers called Lynn Cooper . . .'

'Erm, she's not a teacher, Mr Tick. She's a dinner lady. She works in the kitchen.'

'Ah – of course!' Mr Tick nodded, his eyes blank. 'Her nerves, you say? How frightening can a vegetable rack get? How scary can a deep fryer be?' he chuckled at his own jokes.

Miss Keys just looked at him, baffled.

'I'm wasted here,' he sighed to himself. 'So, off on account of her nerves for the foreseeable future, eh? Hmm . . . We'll have to advertise straight away for a replacement.' He sighed deeply.

Mr Tick pulled his gold-plated fountain pen out of his top pocket and scribbled details of the advertisement on a piece of school notepaper.

The pen left huge blobs on the paper that dribbled as he handed the sheet to Miss Keys.

'There you go! Type this up ASAP, Miss Keys! We can't have the school kitchen grinding to a halt, can we? We'll end up with one of those fussy celebrity chefs swooping down on the school and banging on about healthy eating if we're not careful!' he chuckled.

Miss Keys looked even more confused.

Mr Tick rubbed his forehead wearily. 'The advertisement, please?' he sighed.

Miss Keys scampered off to her desk and began to type. She read the words carefully and checked them twice. She pressed 'print'. At that moment, Mr Tick took a huge slurp of his coffee and realised it had gone cold. Gagging, he shouted for Miss Keys. 'This coffee is cold! Really, Miss Keys! This will not do!'

The secretary scurried off to the coffee machine and rushed back in to the headmaster's office with a steaming fresh cup. A gust of wind pushed its way in through the open window. It tickled the papers on Miss Keys's desk, lingering over the advertisement.

Then, caught by the wind, the advertisement flew into the air and danced out of the window, eventually coming to rest on the sports field.

Miss Keys stumbled back to her desk, pink-cheeked and embarrassed. Fancy letting Mr Tick's coffee get cold! *I hope Lynn's nerves aren't catching!* she shuddered.

She reached for the advertisement. It wasn't there.

I could have sworn I'd printed that already Miss Keys shivered, closing the window against the chill.

CHAPTER 2
WORMING IN

That evening, Ambrose Harbottle and Lady Grimes, two of the plague-pit ghosts who haunted the school, were looking for somewhere to take an evening stroll.

'As beautiful as these dripping sewers are, my love, I feel they are a little . . . *busy*,' said Ambrose, as the Headless Horseman thundered past for the third time. 'Shall we go up above for a quiet walk? The children and teachers have all gone home and the school is quiet.'

'What a *lovely* idea!' Lady Grimes sighed.

Ambrose collected his jar of leeches from a shelf. 'In case we need a picnic!' he grinned.

The school sports field was washed with silver moonlight. Pinpricks of light glowed in the distance. The smell of the sewage-treatment plant drifted across the field.

'In our day, there were no lights from the town, were there, Ambrose?' said Lady Grimes. 'They look so pretty. Just like fireflies.'

'Not as pretty as you, my lovely!' Ambrose grinned. 'Aye, the lay of the land was different then. The town, some small villages, farms dotted here and there – but plenty of places for a leech merchant to ply his noble trade.' Ambrose bowed theatrically.

Lady Grimes smiled and curtsied in return.

'I remember calling at a farm down there –' Ambrose pointed – 'to deliver a pot of leeches to a family. The granddad had boils and they were worried it was the Black Death. When I got

15

there, he staggered out to meet me, dripping pus – I was terrified. I was thinking I'd be a dead man if he *was* infected!' He stopped and stroked Lady Grimes's hand.

'Anyway, turns out when I get a closer look at the old fella that he's just been picking a few old scabs and they've got infected! No Black Death after all! The family were so happy that they gave me this neckerchief as well as my fee.' He fondled a ragged red scarf tied round his grimy neck.

'And very smart it is, too,' Lady Grimes sighed, her eyes shining in the moonlight.

'Ooh – those eyes of yours! A man could sink into those hollow, dark pools! They set off your pale beauty perfectly. And those eyelashes like weed in a drowning pool – so lovely!' Lady Grimes smiled adoringly at Ambrose. He touched her cheek. 'And your skin is so soft and chalky white . . . the colour of powdered bone. Beautiful!'

A tiny spider had been making a web in Lady Grimes's ear. As Ambrose whispered sweet nothings, the spider was disturbed by icy breath. It swung down from her ear like a furry earring on a silken thread, moonlight glittering on its web.

Lady Grimes lowered her eyes shyly to the ground. Ambrose dug his fingers into the mud, making slurping and sucking noises as he moved clods of wet soil.

At last, he found what he was looking for. A fat earthworm pulsed in his hand. He took Lady Grimes's hand in his and gently wound the sticky worm round her finger. It coiled and wriggled wetly, leaving a trail of slime.

'Oh! How un-unusual!' Lady Grimes stuttered.

The worm realised it was somewhere cool and comfortable and dug its head deep into an old wound in her hand to settle down for a nap. It left a coil of its body curled round her finger like a tiny brown rubber ring.

Out of the corner of her eye, Lady Grimes
saw a piece of paper flapping in the breeze.
She picked it up, and her eyes flicked across
the writing.

The worm shifted nervously on her hand. She
stroked it gently and stuffed the paper into her
pocket without giving it another thought.

CHAPTER 3
WORTH NOTING

As the sun rose over the playing fields, Lady Grimes stretched and held her arm out in front of her face, admiring the gently squirming ring on her hand. The worm caught the light of the rising sun and glowed red and gold.

'It's beautiful, Ambrose — thank you so much,' she smiled. 'I think we should be getting back now, my dear. We don't want to still be here when there are herds of boys and girls charging up and down the field chasing a ball! It's all so different from my day, when girls spent their

time pressing flowers and learning how to be
good wives. I love the idea of all the freedom
the girls have, running about . . .' She sighed.

'Well, it's never too late!' grinned Ambrose.
'Off you go – I'm after you!'

Lady Grimes giggled and zoomed off across
the sports field. Ambrose roared along behind her.

'Gotcha!' he grunted, as he swooped to catch
her ribbons.

Lady Grimes spun in the air and Ambrose
missed, then gave chase again.

When they got to the manhole cover, they
were still giggling like children. Oozing down
it, they surprised a rat who was enjoying an
early-morning snack of rotting rice pudding
stolen from the kitchen bins.

The rodent squealed and sprang into the air
in fright. When it landed, the pair had gone.
It scratched its head, puzzled and went back
to its greasy green treat.

Down in the sewer, Ambrose and Lady Grimes popped out next to Edith Codd – ringleader of the plague-pit ghosts – still laughing.

'Oh, young love. How *wonderful*,' Edith sneered. 'Where have you been? What have you been up to? As if I didn't know. Mooning about on the field – yuck! There are far more important things to be doing – like making mischief on the school and all of its awful inhabitants!' She pulled her lips tightly together. Ambrose was suddenly reminded of an old alley cat's bottom as he saw her mouth tighten. He smiled to himself.

'What have you got to smile about? Some of us have been busy while you have been off gallivanting.'

Ambrose's shoulders sagged. Real life – or afterlife – had a way of muscling in and taking the shine off happiness.

Lady Grimes caught his eye and smiled. She held out her hand towards Edith, determined to wipe the cruel smirk off the old hag's face. 'Look! Ambrose gave me this last night. Isn't it wonderful?'

'A *hand*?' Edith sneered. 'He gave you a *hand*? Well, that's the strangest love token I've ever seen!'

Lady Grimes pulled her hand back and looked at her fingers. The worm ring had gone!

'Oh, Ambrose! It must have wriggled away somewhere! I'm so sorry! I wouldn't lose my lovely ring for the world!'

'Don't worry, my dearest – we'll find the little devil! I never have much trouble with finding escaped leeches, and this fella's much bigger and juicier!' said Ambrose, patting her arm. He began crawling around in the sludge, making strange slurping noises.

'What are you doing, you stupid ghost?' Edith barked.

'Worm calling,' said Ambrose, looking at Edith as though she was the stupid one for asking.

'It's like a leech call, but wetter. It's all in the lips
. . .' he said, smacking his own together. A hail
of spittle hit Edith in the eye. She wiped it with
a ragged hankie.

'Sorry I ever asked,' she groaned. Then her
beady eyes glistened as they spotted something
small and brown hanging off one of Lady
Grimes's ribbons. She snatched it off and put
her hand behind her back.

'Perhaps it's in my pocket . . .' Lady Grimes
said, rummaging in the folds of her velvet skirt
for her little pouch. She pulled out the piece of
paper she'd found on the school field.

'What's that?' Edith demanded, rudely.

'Oh, it's just a scrap of paper, Edith,' Ambrose
replied. He was more interested in finding the
worm ring and making Lady Grimes happy
again.

Edith stared at Lady Grimes. She looked away
and screwed up the paper, trying to hide it again

in her pocket, but Edith grabbed her wrist with
her free hand.

'I *said*, what's that?' she growled.

'Nothing, Edith . . . I told you . . .' said Ambrose.

'I can see that it *is* something by the look on your lady love's face, Ambrose. What are you hiding from me?'

Ambrose just looked puzzled. He wasn't hiding anything. Why couldn't Edith ever concentrate on important matters instead of her own mean little schemes?

'We're trying to find Lady Grimes's ring, Edith. That's the important thing right now . . .' he said, slowly, as though she was a small child.

'And *I'm* trying to find out what Lady Grimes is hiding. I'll take that, thank you!' She snatched the paper away from Lady Grimes. She held it up to her face and smoothed it out, squinting at the writing.

'You're holding the paper upside down,' Lady Grimes said, icily. 'I know you can't read, Edith. Give it back, if you please.' She held out an elegant hand.

'Actually, I *don't* please,' Edith spat angrily. 'I want you to read it out, now. I want to know what it is, NOW!'

'I'm sorry, Edith. I simply just cannot do that. I suggest you return the paper to me and be done with it,' sighed Lady Grimes, brushing imaginary dust casually from her sleeve. She looked at Edith as though she was a bothersome servant.

'I suppose you don't want this, then . . .' smiled Edith, cruelly. She held Lady Grimes's precious worm ring on the wrinkly palm of her hand. It writhed unhappily.

'Edith! Please return my ring!' Lady Grimes demanded, thrusting a hand out in front of her. The worm stretched towards safety.

'You had the ring the whole time!' scowled Ambrose.

Edith pulled a face at him. 'In the words of the bratty children up above – *well, duh!*' she laughed, rudely. 'Now, read the note.'

26

Lady Grimes frowned. 'Very well, Edith.' She raised her chin and looked down her nose at the thin, wispy-haired woman. 'The note, please.'

Edith passed the piece of paper over, sticking out her tongue triumphantly.

'It says, "Required: temporary dinner lady to cover for sickness. Good rates of pay; excellent position for right person." Satisfied, Edith? My ring now, please.'

Edith thrust the worm into Lady Grimes's hand. It curled happily around her finger again, and went straight to sleep.

'Dinner lady, eh? Hmmm . . . I can work with that! There's some organising to do . . . but now I have a plan to close down St Sebastian's School for good!' she cackled.

She threw her head back and danced a little jig of glee, pointy elbows and knees jabbing the air viciously. A cloud of flakes flew off her scaly cheeks and whirled around her in the air like a

snowstorm. Her eyes glowed a sickly green from
the centre of the whirlwind.

'Here we go again . . .' Ambrose groaned.

CHAPTER 4
MONSTER MAYHEM

A week later, Miss Keys's office was fizzing with activity. Three people were waiting nervously to be called in to interview for Mrs Cooper's job with Mr Tick. The secretary fluttered backwards and forwards, filling coffee cups and rearranging papers and references for the umpteenth time.

There had been lots of phone calls enquiring about the position, but many of the applicants had been put off when they realised the school involved was St Sebastian's. One strange man had even suggested that the building was haunted!

Miss Keys giggled and shook her head to herself. What had he said? Oh, yes – 'I couldn't be doing with a job where I had to exorcise the kitchen every day before I started work'!

In all, eight people had been for a tour of the kitchen, but several of those had been weird. Miss Keys shuddered as she remembered the lady who had swept round the kitchen smelling of incense, shaking a crystal on a chain and talking about 'bad vibrations'. She'd given Miss Keys the creeps! She'd skidded to a halt in front of the store cupboard and refused point blank to go any further. Strange.

Then there had been the woman who had insisted she kept seeing things out of the corner of her eye as she'd looked round the kitchen. She'd jumped and squealed so many times that she'd made Miss Keys a nervous wreck. She couldn't seem to get away from St Sebastian's fast enough after the tour.

Miss Keys looked round at the final selection sitting in her office. They seemed a little nervous, but otherwise solid and dependable.

There was Gareth Fleet, an ex-army cook. *He looks completely unflappable,* thought Miss Keys, *with his straight back and strong, muscly arms. I bet he doesn't stand for any nonsense!* The man looked at her and smiled.

Then there was Liz Brodie. *She seems like a lovely, motherly woman,* thought Miss Keys. *I expect she'd have the kitchen organised in a moment. If she can look after six children and still find time to cook for*

the children at St Sebastian's she must be a whirlwind.
The woman caught Miss Keys's eye and beamed
at her. *She seems so warm and friendly too* . . . Miss
Keys lost herself in a daydream of being brought
freshly baked treats by the plump little woman.

Coming back to the real world, Miss Keys
looked at the third applicant, Penny Grub. She
was young and perky, and was looking around
the room, flicking her long blonde hair and smiling

prettily at everyone. Her eyes glittered brightly
and she almost seemed to fizz with energy.

*She looks a bit like a children's TV presenter from
one of those noisy Saturday morning shows*, thought
Miss Keys. *She's the one who's worked as a TV chef
. . . interesting.* The secretary's thoughts were
drifting again.

She went to pour yet more coffee and found
the milk jug was empty. 'Won't be a moment!
Just off to get some milk from the staffroom
fridge!' she smiled.

The candidates were too busy secretly trying
to stare at each other to take much notice.
Miss Keys swept out of the room carrying the
milk jug.

The room was silent. Each candidate seemed
to be concentrating on their notes, or looking
for something in their bags, but they took every
opportunity to size each other up, rating their
chances against each other.

He looks nice . . . but a fella? How can he take charge of a kitchen? thought Mrs Brodie, looking at Mr Fleet. She smiled as she remembered the state her kitchen had been in last Mother's Day, when her husband, Steve, had helped the children make lunch. *I was cleaning up spills for a week!* She chuckled to herself. *And that girl is far too young for a post like this,* she thought, as she sneaked a look at Miss Grub.

Suddenly, the office door flew open. Mrs Brodie turned towards it. 'Can I help you with making the coffees Miss Ke . . . aargh!'

A huge, scaly monster filled the doorway. Its enormous hands ended in barbed claws that scratched at the air. Its skin seemed to move as though tiny creatures crawled in the folds.

As it walked towards the candidates, it left puddles of glowing sludge on the floor. They steamed, and the air was filled with a warm, fishy smell.

It opened its mouth, showing teeth like huge needles and a black, forked tongue. As it breathed, purple and red flames licked out of its mouth.

The candidates sat frozen, staring at the monster. Their eyes saw it – and their noses certainly smelt it – but their brains could not believe it. The only sound in the room was the harsh breathing of the beast, and the ticking of the clock on the wall.

Mr Fleet was the first to react. 'It's . . . it's . . . a m–m–monster!' he shrieked, leaping up and flinging papers everywhere.

The monster turned to look at him. 'Eat . . . you . . .' it growled, reaching towards him. Its voice sounded like a metal blade scraping over gravel.

'What the devil *is* that thing?' Mrs Brodie screeched, pinging up out of her seat and hiding behind the coat stand.

'I don't need a job *this* badly!' shouted Mr Fleet, running for the door.

Mrs Brodie and Miss Grub beat him to it and, for one horrible moment, they all jammed in the doorway.

The monster shambled closer until they felt its hot, smelly breath on their skin. Then, like a cork whizzing out of a bottle, they shot out of the doorway and thundered towards the school entrance.

The monster staggered after them growling, 'Eat . . . them . . .', strings of drool slithering from its jaws.

Stopping at the entrance, it raised its nose into the air and sniffed. Green snot bubbled in its nostrils.

'I smell them . . .' it hissed, as it stumbled down the front steps and away from the building.

Miss Keys came back into the room carrying a jug of milk.

'Here we go. Oh! – where's everybody gone?'

Miss Grub crossed her legs and looked at Miss Keys, flicking her long, blonde hair over her shoulder. Edith had worked very hard to get her impersonation of Penny Grub just right. It had been difficult to morph into just the right shape, and she'd had to study the woman on the caretaker's magic picture box hard. *What did he call it?* she strained to remember. *Ah, yes! A teevee.*

'Uh – they had to step out *for a bite.*' Edith flicked her Miss Grub hair again, smiling sweetly.

At that moment, Mr Tick buzzed the intercom. 'Send in the first candidate, please, Miss Keys.'

Miss Keys frowned, puzzled. She looked behind the coat stand, as though she expected the other candidates to be hiding there.

Mr Tick, impatient at being kept waiting, marched out of his office and thrust a hand towards Miss Grub.

'Pleased to meet you,' he smiled. He looked past Miss Grub at Miss Keys. 'Where are the others?' he mouthed. Miss Keys shrugged.

Neither of them was looking at Miss Grub. If they had been, they would have noticed something strange about her eyes. They were glowing with an eerie, red light.

CHAPTER 5
WELCOME NEWS

*Hmmm, I'm sure there were supposed to be three
candidates today,* Mr Tick thought to himself. *Miss
Keys doesn't seem to know what's going on – I'll have
to speak to her about her lack of organisation later.
Still, this one looks bright and perky enough!*

'Come in, have a seat,' he smiled, ushering Miss
Grub into his office. He pointed at a low chair in
front of his desk. He sat the other side on a high,
leather upholstered chair.

Miss Keys sighed. *He looks like a king on his
throne,* she thought as she carried a tray of drinks

40

in to the room and put them down on the desk. She handed a 'St Sebastian's – A First Class Education!' mug to Miss Grub. Mr Tick's coffee was in his favourite 'Solitaire Champion' mug, specially scoured clean for the occasion.

'Right! Down to business!' Mr Tick smiled. He flicked his fingers at his secretary. 'We won't be needing you just now, Miss Keys. I shall call if I want anything.'

Miss Keys's shoulders sagged. She left the office quietly.

'Now, let's see . . .' said Mr Tick as he shuffled papers on his desk, thinking it made him look busy and important.

'I am very keen to fill this position quickly. I have been left in a most inconvenient situation here, with only one dinner lady.' He spread his hands out to express his disbelief. 'I know people get sick, but *nerves*? There's nothing here at St Sebastian's to make a person nervous!' he laughed.

He looked at Miss Grub's job-application form. 'I see you have quite a bit of experience. Good, good. Tell me a bit more about yourself. Are you used to working under pressure? Can't have another dinner lady cracking up. Ha, ha! – just my little joke . . .' he smiled thinly. 'Can you manage staff if required? I place great importance on good management – obviously!' he preened, straightening his tie.

'Yes, indeed, sire,' Miss Grub grinned, revealing a set of stained, brown teeth that would have put an old pirate to shame.

Good grief – look at that mouth! And her breath's a bit wiffy . . . Mr Tick thought to himself. He shifted uncomfortably on his chair. Funny accent too, he thought. *Who makes 'sir' sound like 'sire'? Oh, well – beggars can't be choosers, I suppose* . . .

'Could you tell me about some of your favourite recipes? "Signature dishes", I think you chefs call them.' He smiled smugly to himself, always happy to show off his general knowledge.

'Well, sire, they are many,' replied Miss Grub.

There she goes again with the weird language,
Mr Tick thought. He frowned slightly, feeling
rather puzzled.

'My pantry is always well stocked with specially
gathered herbs. I like to make my concoctions as
tasty as possible!' she continued, grinning again.

Mr Tick quickly closed his eyes. Too late; the sight of her rotten teeth was already burnt on to the insides of his eyelids like a photograph.

'The little ones will love my armoured turnips, and my compost is second to none!' Miss Grub put her fingers to her lips and made a weird kissing sound to let Mr Tick know how delicious her cooking was. Unfortunately, it made him feel vaguely sick, since it made him think of her teeth again.

'"Compost"? Don't you mean *c-compote*?' he stuttered.

'Ha, ha! You are so funny – of course I mean compost – you know, root vegetables, like carrots baked in vinegar!' she laughed.

Must be one of those celebrity-chef meals, Mr Tick thought. *Oh, well, a bit fancy for school, but at least she has some new ideas – could win me some points at the town hall . . .*

Miss Grub was warming to her subject.

'My frumenty pudding always wins praise, and there's my baked mallard and venison custarde . . .'

'All very delicious, I'm sure!' blustered Mr Tick. He was starting to feel rather out of his depth. He had fancied himself as a bit of an expert on fine cooking, as a result of his frequent trips to the Funky Ferret Gastropub down the road. This woman had him beaten. *I blame all this new-fangled TV cooking, he thought. Still – she sounds as though she knows what's she's talking about – and we're desperate. I suppose it all boils down to meat and two veg in the end.*

'Well, Miss Grub – what an appropriate name, ha, ha! – I am delighted to tell you that you've got the job!' said Mr Tick, leaping up and shaking her vigorously by the hand. *Of course, it helps that she seems to be the only candidate*, he thought to himself. 'Congratulations! Now, let's go and introduce you to your colleague in the kitchen!'

He ushered Miss Grub out of his office, through the school's back entrance and across the playground into the kitchen. *The sooner this is over, the better,* he thought. *Then I can get back to more important matters; there's a solitaire game I need to finish!*

As they entered the kitchen, Mrs Meadows was stirring sponge mix with one hand and mashing potato with the other.

'Ahem,' said Mr Tick, in order to get her attention. He couldn't remember her name. 'This is your new colleague, Miss Grub.'

'Am I glad to see you!' Mrs Meadows sighed. She rubbed her hands on her apron, straightened her cap, coming forwards to shake hands.

'It gladdens my heart to meet you too, sister!' Miss Grub answered, bobbing a small curtsey.

She's an odd one. Still, I'd welcome the Wicked Witch of the West today if she had a spare pair of hands! thought Mrs Meadows, trying to smile.

46

'Lovely!' exclaimed Mr Tick, clapping his hands. 'Have a good look round and get your bearings, Miss Grub. I'm sure Mrs erm . . . er . . .'

'Meadows, sir.'

'Absolutely – of course – Mrs *Meadows* will show you the ropes. You can start properly tomorrow.'

'Ropes, sire? For hanging game and meat? Wonderful! I am sure I shall learn quickly,' said Miss Grub, curtseying again.

Mr Tick smiled weakly and swept from kitchen, heading for the comfort of his solitaire game.

This should be interesting, thought Mrs Meadows. 'Right! Let's put the kettle on!' she said, smiling at Miss Grub. 'Have a sit-down.'

She made a pot of tea and poured out two steaming mugsfuls. 'I'll just get some biscuits from the store cupboard!' she smiled.

As Mrs Meadows left the room, Miss Grub dug about in her pocket and pulled out a little bottle with a picture of a zombie on it.

47

'This'll soon have her doing whatever I tell her!' Miss Grub whispered to herself, as removed the stopper and poured a couple of drops into the steaming liquid inside Mrs Meadows's mug.

CHAPTER 6
RECIPE FOR DISASTER

Edith skipped back into the sewer, cackling with excitement. As she ran, she morphed back from Miss Grub into her usual form. The long, silky blonde hair changed to Edith's wispy red. The soft, pink cheeks withered, and the cute, turned-up nose curled over in to a hook.

'I've done it! I've got the job!' she shouted. 'That stupid headmaster has played right into my hands and made me a dinner lady at St Sebastian's! Now I'll be able to close the whole place down by myself – by poisoning all the pupils! If they're gone, the school will have to close down – *forever*!'

Edith danced across to a shelf. She rummaged about amongst the skulls, old candle stubs and cobwebs until she found a basket.

'I'll start collecting ingredients straight away, so I can start my poisoning spree tomorrow! Hmmm, the question is, slow and painful or sudden strike? A quick-acting poison would empty the school fast, but no one would suffer very much. And, oh, how those pupils deserve to suffer! The headaches their trampling feet have caused . . .' she slapped her hand to her forehead, causing a flurry of flakes to fall from her face.

Dusting her hand off on her skirt, Edith sank on to a chair made of thigh bones. 'The stress they've given me, they deserve to suffer! Slow and painful – tee hee!'

She jumped up again – her decision made – and started collecting things in her basket.

'Powdered bone – that'll choke them! I'll make some nice cakes with bone flour.' She snatched up some bones and dropped them into her basket, ready to grind into powder in the school kitchen.

'Now, what else? Ooh! I know, some sludge added to a sloppy pudding – that'll sicken their stomachs! Excellent!'

Edith scooped up a blob of stinking brown sludge off the floor using a skull with its jaw missing and added that to her basket, too.

Several flies buzzed round the sludge. Edith caught them in her hand and trapped them in a piece of rag. 'These will do in the place of raisins – bound to make them sick!' she cackled, rubbing her hands together.

She felt along a high shelf, and her cold hand closed around a sleeping rat. It woke with a terrified squeak as Edith pulled it off the shelf. It was so scared that it left a pile of rat poo on her hand as it leapt away to safety.

Edith looked at the poo and smiled. 'I'll add this to the dumplings – extra flavour! With a bit of luck, it'll give the children a horrible disease.' She dropped the poo into her basket.

'What else? Hmmm . . .' Edith pushed aside a heap of rags with her foot. She found a skull squirming with maggots. '*Lovely!* I'll have some of those. I can add them to the rice pudding!

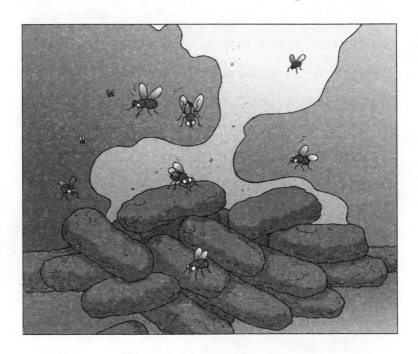

I can't wait to see the kiddies spooning wriggling rice into their mouths!'

She laughed so hard, she had a coughing fit. She spluttered into a rag, examined the contents and popped it into her basket. 'Might come in handy for thickening stews!' she smiled. 'I can't wait to get started! Imagine all those sick, green faces . . . the groaning and the moaning. It'll be sweet music to my ears! And I'll cook something extra-specially nasty for that stupid headmaster.'

She rubbed her hands together, sending a shower of skin flakes sailing to the floor that buried a passing cockroach up to its antennae. It was startled, but then settled down for a good munch. The crunching sounds attracted a crowd of other roaches.

Edith spotted them, scooped them up in some toilet paper and threw them into her basket as well. 'If I squash them a bit, they'll look just like dates!' she giggled.

At that moment, Ambrose, along with William
Scroggins, burst back into the amphitheatre.

'That was fun, Ambrose!' William laughed,
his hair sticking out at funny angles. 'I'm so glad

football isn't against the law at St Sebastian's! I saw it played once while I was alive but the soldiers came and broke it up – people were bleeding all over the place and a couple of legs got broken. At least our game didn't cause any damage!'

'Speak for yourself!' laughed the Headless Horseman, galloping in. 'It was my head we were using as a ball!' He tweaked his nose, which was looking a bit flat, back into shape.

Ambrose was puffing and blowing. He eased himself down on to a bench made from bones. 'Well, William, lad – that was good fun but I'm worn out!' he grinned.

The smile slipped from his face as he noticed Edith collecting things in a basket. He nudged William. 'What do you think she's up to? Looks like she's got another plan brewing.'

Edith was cackling, still throwing 'ingredients' into her basket.

'Edith – what are you doing?' William asked.

Edith rushed towards them, waving her basket.
'I have a wonderful plan – it can't go wrong! I
fooled that ridiculous headmaster into giving me
a job. I'm the new dinner lady at St Sebastian's
School!' she grinned round at the other ghosts.
Ambrose looked puzzled.

'Good . . . I suppose . . .?' he looked at William.
William shrugged. Edith sighed heavily.

'Isn't it *obvious*? I'm going to poison the food!'

William's mouth dropped open.

'That's right, William – be amazed. It's a great
plan, isn't it?'

William's mouth fell shut again.

'I've collected lots of ingredients – look!' Edith
lifted various items out of the basket.

'Sludge, roaches – oh! Where have they gone?'
She shook the toilet paper and looked
underneath it. She screwed it up and threw it on
the floor. 'Oh, never mind! We'll find some more.

There's a job for you, William! And here are some flies . . . and some rat poo!' she giggled.

William frowned.

Edith was so excited that she didn't notice, and skipped off. 'I'll be back when the basket's full!' she called over her shoulder.

William grabbed at his friend's sleeve. 'Ambrose, we can't let her do this! We can't let her poison everyone in the school!'

'Calm down, son!' Ambrose said, patting William's arm gently. 'Think about it. All those things Edith has collected – they might make people sick, but they're not actually *poisonous*. Even if she did manage to get anything into the food – which I doubt – someone might get an upset belly but no one's going to die.'

'Are you sure, Ambrose? What if she really hurts someone?' William whispered. He looked down at the floor. He loved St Sebastian's. It was the closest thing to school he'd ever known, not ever having had the chance to go in his short lifetime.

'Cheer up, lad! No one's getting hurt around here!' said Ambrose.

'Don't you think we should try and stop her?' William asked. 'We could —'

'Edith won't listen to us, William,' interrupted Ambrose. 'You know her, once she has a scheme in her head, that's it. I think we just sit back and wait. You'll see.'

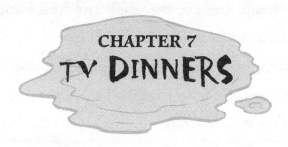

CHAPTER 7
TV DINNERS

'Come on, Stick – you can do it – ohhh!'

James Simpson and Lenny Maxwell were trying to teach Alexander Tick how to ride a skateboard. The three boys all lived close by to one another, so they usually walked to and from school together. Today, the journey was taking twice as long as usual because Alexander kept falling off James's board.

'Sorry! I just can't keep my balance. My mind knows the theory – I'm counterbalancing my weight – but my body simply refuses to cooperate!' said Alexander, as he got up off the ground after his latest wipeout.

'You'll get there in the end!' laughed James.

'In an ambulance?' joked Alexander. By the time the school gates were in sight, he was dusty and bruised. 'I'd better go and smarten myself up!' he grinned.

'Where do you think you're off to, young man?' said Mr Hall, the history teacher, stopping Alexander in his tracks.

'To tidy myself up, sir.'

'No time for that now. Mr Tick wants you all into assembly sharpish this morning – he says he has some very exciting news!' the teacher smiled. 'I would have thought you'd know all about that already, Alexander!'

James and Lenny turned to Alexander.

'What news?' James said, rubbing his hands together and coming closer. 'School's not closing early for the holidays, is it?'

'Or maybe they're filming a reality TV show? – *I'm A Schoolboy – Get Me Out Of Here!*' laughed Lenny.

Alexander shuffled and looked awkward.

'Sorry, guys – I did know, but Dad made me promise not to say anything . . . he'll go mad if I spill the beans.' His hand flew to his mouth. 'Uh-oh! I've gone and given you a clue without meaning to!'

'Ve haf veys of making you talk . . .' James grabbed Alexander's arm. 'Ve shall torture it out of you if necessary . . . tickling ze armpits usually vorks . . .' He advanced on Alexander, his fingers waggling in front of him.

'I can't – I promised!' Alexander wailed.

James dropped his arms to his sides and rolled his eyes.

'Oh, all right, don't get your knickers in a twist. I suppose we'll find out soon enough with everyone else . . .'

Mr Hall ushered the boys along and they shuffled into assembly with everyone else. They found their places and sat down.

Mr Drew, the music teacher, was sitting at the piano playing a tune as they filed in. Mr Watts, the science teacher, had told him research had proven that playing music as pupils came into assembly kept them calm. However, Mr Drew was playing a medley of punk anthems from his youth. He'd been in a band called The Rotten Rejects and he remembered his glory days with affection. The result was not soothing *at all*.

'Wow, Mr Drew's got fingers like lightning!' said Alexander.

James looked at him with his mouth hanging open. 'Eh?'

'They never strike in the same place twice!' Alexander giggled.

Lenny laughed out loud, earning a scowl from Mr Tick. The boys settled down.

'Thank you, Mr Drew . . .' Mr Tick shouted over the music.

Lost back in 1977, Mr Drew carried on smashing his fingers down on the keyboards. He was remembering the crowds – well, twelve people including his baffled-looking mum – pogo-ing up and down to his band's music . . .

'MR DREW! I SAID THANK YOU!' Mr Tick bellowed across the hall.

The music teacher was jolted back to the present. He smiled apologetically at the headmaster. A few sniggers from pupils were quietened by a stare from Mr Tick. The headmaster then smiled and clapped his hands together.

'I have wonderful news!' he announced. He looked around the hall with a huge grin on his face.

'What do you reckon? A visit from an astronaut?' whispered Lenny.

'Or maybe your dad's been promoted to work in the town hall – and we'll get a new headmaster!' James hissed. Alexander turned to glare at his friend. James gave him a weak smile.

Mr Tick cleared his throat. 'Never let it be said that St Sebastian's doesn't attract staff of the very highest standard . . .'

James looked down the line of teachers sitting along the side of the hall. Mr Hall was trying to pick his nose without anyone noticing and Mr Watts was staring out of the window, obviously bored. Mr Drew was flirting with Ms Legg, the PE teacher. He was smiling and winking so often he looked as though he had a facial tic.

Yeah, the very highest standard — not! James thought.

'We are very fortunate to welcome a new dinner lady to our school – Miss Penny Grub – star of *Grub's Grub* television show!' He looked around the hall with his arms raised, as though he was waiting for a round of applause.

The hall was silent. Pupils and teachers looked at each other, confused. Everyone whispered among themselves. Nobody had heard of the show, let alone the 'star'.

Frowning slightly, Mr Tick continued. 'So, nothing but gourmet dinners from now on! I look forward to hearing how delighted you are in due course. Right! We all have a very busy day ahead of us, so I shall leave you in the capable hands of your form tutors!' He scooted down from the podium and rushed off to his office, Miss Keys trailing in his wake.

'Ungrateful lot!' Mr Tick spat. 'Top-notch food literally handed to them on a plate and they're *still* not happy.'

Back in the hall, James, Lenny and Alexander were waiting in line to leave.

'I can't believe *that's* all the fabulous news was!' Lenny muttered.

'I know!' James rolled his eyes. 'We should have known not to get our hopes up!'

'But it'll be great!' Alexander protested. 'I've seen her show on satellite TV. She cooks really interesting food!'

'Oh, dear, "interesting" food. That reminds me of the time my mum decided to go on a Chinese cookery course. "Interesting" was the word Dad used when we tried what she'd made. Miss Grub can keep her fancy food,' James groaned. 'What's wrong with good, old-fashioned pizza and chips, I ask you?'

'Mmm . . . nothing!' said Lenny. 'Except you're making me hungry . . .'

'It's only nine-thirty, Lenny! I know your mum makes you eat belly-busting breakfasts because

I've stayed at your house. How can you be hungry *already*?' said James.

'My Dad says it's because I'm a growing lad,' Lenny laughed.

'Blimey – I hope not – unless you see a bright future as a basketball star!' James replied, ducking as Lenny swiped at the air where his head had been.

'Well, I think you're both in for a lovely surprise,' Alexander smiled, smugly. 'And I'm going to ask Miss Grub for her autograph when I see her.'

'Creep!' James exclaimed, dissolving into fits of laughter. Mr Hall scowled at him and he tried to stifle his chortling.

'Hey, Stick,' Lenny whispered. 'You could ask her to autograph your pizza . . .'

Alexander scowled.

'Just you wait and see. You'll be amazed by what this woman can do in the kitchen!' he huffed.

CHAPTER 8
AYE, EYE!

After maths with Mr Parker, the boys' next lesson was double French with Madame Dupont. As they took their seats, they saw photographs and posters of cafés and restaurants taped to the board.

'Today, we are going to talk about ordering a meal at a café or restaurant,' she smiled. Alexander rubbed his hands together and then shot a hand into the air.

'Madame Dupont? Did you know that the famous TV chef Penny Grub has come to work at the school as a dinner lady?' His eyes shone.

'But, yes, Alexandre. I had heard this and it is excellent news, no? We shall see some fantastic dishes at lunchtime, I think!' She turned to the board. 'Now class —'

'Madame Dupont?' interrupted Alexander. 'Do you think she'll cook *pot-au-feu*? I saw Miss Grub make that live on TV once and it looked delicious!'

'I certainly hope so! It would remind me so much of the meals my *grandmere* used to cook for our family . . .' replied Madame Dupont, looking all misty-eyed.

'Pot of fur? Wossat?' hissed James.

Lenny looked alarmed.

'It's a beef stew; quite literally, the name means "pot on the fire". It's quite delicious and superior by far to . . .' Alexander trailed off.

James had interrupted him by sticking out his tongue.

'OK, professor — too much information, ta!'

Alexander continued to drone on about different sorts of French cooking with Madame Dupont, who was lost in descriptions of meals she had enjoyed at her grandmother's table in France.

The rest of the class was growing restless. Some boys at the back were flicking broken bits of a plastic pencil case round the room with rulers. A piece hit Lenny on the neck.

'Ow! That hurt!' he shrieked, leaping in the air and rubbing his neck.

Madame Dupont spun round and looked at Lenny, her eyes wide and surprised. She spotted the clock behind him on the wall. It was lunchtime already!

'Very well, children, it is time for you to sample the delights of Mademoiselle Grub's kitchen! We shall return to this topic next time. Alexandre, I shall write down some recipes for you if you will stay behind after class.' She began to scribble them down.

James and Lenny hung around the desk for a while, then grew tired of waiting and drifted out into the corridor.

'This is daft! I'm starving. I want to go and get dinner, not wait around here,' moaned Lenny.

'Me too!' grumbled James.

At that moment, Gordon 'The Gorilla' Carver – St Sebastian's resident bully – trundled up to them. Leaning round the door of the French classroom, he overheard Alexander and Madame Dupont's conversation.

'Waiting for Little Chef, are you?' he snorted. 'There'll be no dinner left by the time you two get there if I have anything to do with it!'

James pulled a face as Gordon ran off. At that moment, Alexander skipped out of the room.

'Madame Dupont's given me some great recipes!' He waved a pile of papers. 'She's really given me food for thought. Ha, ha!'

James rolled his eyes.

'Talking of food, can we go down to the canteen and get some? At this rate, we'll miss it all!' he grumbled.

'Oh! Yes – I'd nearly forgotten in all the excitement! Let's get down there before the best things are gone! It's a historic day – a TV chef at St Sebastian's!' He grinned, and the friends ran down the stairs and out across the playground towards the canteen.

The lunch queue was enormous.

'Looks like nobody's bought a packed lunch today!' moaned James. 'I hope it doesn't take too long to get served. I hate it when you wait for ages and all the best stuff's gone.'

'What d'you think it'll be?' asked Lenny, smiling hopefully. 'Something nice like steak and chips?'

'I doubt it, Lenny,' said Alexander, shaking his head. 'Talking of steak, did you know that the only reason vampires like school dinners is because they *know* they won't get a stake. . .'

'Go on – taste it!' Alexander laughed.

Lenny scooped a tiny bit of stew on to his fork and edged it slowly towards his mouth. As he tasted it, a grin spread across his face.

'It's great!' he said through his mouthful. He started to dig in to the large plate of food in front of him.

James was munching happily on his plateful, until he found a stringy piece of gristle. He pulled it out of his mouth, frowning.

'Some of the meat's a bit ropey . . .' he muttered. He looked at Alexander's plate. 'Is yours OK?'

'It's fine, James – better than fine; it's wonderful!' he smiled. 'Quite a triumph for Miss Grub on her first day!'

'How about you, Lenny?' asked James. 'Is your meat OK?' He glanced down at Lenny's plate.

Lenny nodded, lifting another forkful of food to his mouth.

James stared. He could see a round, white lump in the middle of Lenny's fork. The food slid forwards, as Lenny tipped it towards his lips. James jumped as the lump spun round and looked at him.

It was an eyeball!

'Lenny! Don't eat it!' he shrieked.

Lenny dropped the fork with a clatter. 'James! If this is a joke, it's not funny!' he said.

Then he saw the eyeball.

'*Gross!* I could have eaten that!' He shuddered, and his lip curled in disgust. 'Alexander! There's an eyeball in my dinner! And it's staring at me! So much for your Miss Grub's cooking!' He shoved his plate away.

'Well,' said Alexander, 'you must realise that there are cultural differences at play here. The parts of animals we find disgusting to eat can be totally acceptable to people from some other countries, and vice versa. Now, take the traditional tribal food eaten by –'

'Stick. This is beef stew, right?' interrupted James.

'Well, of a sort. It's *pot-au-feu*, remember?' Alexander explained, patiently.

'But the meat's beef?' James persisted.

'It is.'

78

'OK,' said James, poking the eyeball with his fork and turning it towards Alexander. 'Since when did cows have *blue* eyes?'

CHAPTER 9
STAR-STRUCK

'An eyeball. In the stew. In *my* stew.' Lenny was in shock. 'I *knew* I didn't like posh cooking!'

'We'll have to investigate. We need to go down to the kitchen and see what's up. Maybe if we pretend Stick's an autograph hunter, we'll have a way in,' said James.

'I *do* still want an autograph! I'm sure this is all just a silly mistake,' said Alexander. 'However, the kitchens are out of bounds, remember?'

'But we have to find out what's happening,' insisted James. 'What if it's the ghosts up to no

80

good again? We have to know for sure. Anyway, if Miss Grub is a genuine TV chef she's bound to be pleased that somebody wants her autograph. A celebrity with no fans isn't a celebrity, after all!' James crossed his arms and looked at Alexander.

'Well, OK,' Alexander agreed, reluctantly. 'I'm sure we won't find anything weird – and I really *do* want her autograph. It'll have pride of place in my book, between Mr Watts and Professor Crump.'

'Professor Crump? Who's that?' asked Lenny, still frowning at his plate.

'You remember – the famous archaeologist who came to film a documentary in Grimesford about how the Black Death spread to this area in a cart of rat-infested cabbages? It was utterly fascinating.' Alexander went dewy-eyed at the thought. 'I'd love to be just like him when I grow up.'

'Well, anyway – I'm sure she'll be tickled pink that you want her autograph if she's really Penny Grub. It's not like she's a huge star already if she needs a day job at St Sebastian's. And remember – *Grub's Grub* is only on cable. My dad says any old weirdo with a few quid can make a cable show,' said James.

'I don't think Miss Grub comes into *that* category!' Alexander sniffed, snootily. 'I suppose, if we're careful, nobody needs to know we've been anywhere near the kitchens. And her autograph *would* really complete my collection . . .'

The boys took advantage of the crowd inside the canteen to sneak towards the kitchen doors without being seen.

'Yuck! It smells like my grandad's sweaty socks!' moaned Lenny, covering his nose. 'Mixed in with old rotten eggs and stinky drains . . .' His face was already pale from his eyeball adventure. Now it took on a green tinge.

'I expect that's what it is,' said Alexander. 'There's been a lot of rain lately, so perhaps the drains have backed up. My dad does keep telling people not to drop litter in the playground. He works very hard to run a tight ship. Only last week —'

'Shhh!' James interrupted. 'Do you want this autograph or not?' He'd heard Alexander's long moans about how hard his dad had to work before. Privately, he suspected that hard work wasn't the reason why Mr Tick didn't have much time for Alexander, but he kept his ideas to himself.

The boys paused in front of the kitchen door. The sound of pans clattering together and strange muttering came from inside.

James pushed the door open slowly. Miss Grub was bent over a huge vat of green, bubbling soup. She was stirring it with what looked like a branch, and kept reaching into a basket and

pulling items out, dropping them into the
mixture gleefully. The kitchen was full of steam.

James and Lenny edged into the room slowly.

'She looks like an old kitchen maid from one
of those history videos Mr Hall keeps making us
watch . . . Strange,' said James.

Suddenly, the boys were pushed out of the
way by Alexander as he dashed past them,
waving his leather-bound autograph book.
Lenny nudged James.

'That book was a present from his dad – and he'd written his autograph in it before he gave it to him! The sad thing is, Stick would have probably asked for it if it hadn't already been in there . . .'

'I know,' said James, shaking his head. 'Like he said, he's got Mr Watts's autograph in there too. Just being a scientist is enough to make someone a hero in his eyes. We'll have to take him in hand, Lenny, or he's doomed to a lifetime of corduroy trousers and *Open University* re-runs.'

Meanwhile, Alexander was bounding across the kitchen towards Miss Grub.

'I *love* your show,

Miss Grub! I'm a *huge* fan!' gushed Alexander.

Miss Grub looked up, startled. Her cheeks were flushed and her hair was a mess.

'Wow!' James whispered to Lenny. 'Those TV make-up artists must really do a good job – that's not a pretty sight!'

Alexander hadn't noticed. He waved his autograph book and pen. 'Would you mind awfully, Miss Grub? You can use my pen!'

The cook looked at him blankly. *What on earth does that silly boy want? I wish the pesky child would buzz off and let me get on!*

'What do you want me to do?' Miss Grub said, baffled. She grabbed the pen and book and the boy smiled. 'Ah! You want me to make my mark!' she smiled.

Alexander saw her brown, rotten teeth up close and gulped. With her tongue sticking out of the corner of her mouth, the woman grunted and scratched a big 'X' on the page. Alexander's eyes goggled.

'Er . . . Miss Grub . . .?' he mumbled. Then a horrible thought struck him. *Miss Grub can't write! Surely a TV chef would be able to write . . . Oh, no!*

His eyes slid towards James and Lenny. James had his arms crossed.

'Ghost!' he mouthed, waving his fingers as
though he were haunting the kitchen himself.
The room was silent except for the bubbling,
gassy noises coming from the vat.

'Right, if you'll excuse me, I must get on!'
Miss Grub flapped about the kitchen like a
startled chicken, snatching up pans, spoons
and ingredients.

'Erm . . . where's Mrs Meadows?' asked James.

'Having a well-deserved break from you children!' snapped Miss Grub. For a moment, her features seemed to be fluid, shifting slightly.

James blinked, and the illusion was gone. Miss Grub was patting down her hair and smiling.

'Now, boys – I'll never get all these meals prepared if we stand around chatting! It's been lovely to meet you but I'm rather busy.' She started hauling piles of sticks towards the oven and stacked them inside.

The boys watched in stunned silence. She took a pouch from her pocket and began to light a fire. As she fanned the flames, James pointed at the door. The boys crept out and ran back across the playground.

'Well, I don't think there's any doubt about it now, guys – our new dinner lady is no TV chef,' puffed James, as he skidded to a halt outside the main doors.

Alexander looked crushed.

'Poor Dad! He'll be so disappointed.'

'Never mind that! We need to find out why there's a ghost posing as a dinner lady in the school kitchens, and what she's up to . . .'

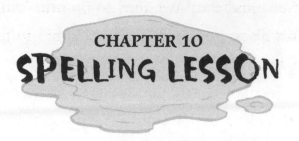

That night, an exhausted Edith slid back down into the sewers. As soon as the school had closed, she had made her escape.

She staggered into the amphitheatre, shreds of her Miss Grub disguise still clinging to her. Her pink skin gradually sank and dried, taking on the appearance of an old prune, and she sank into her chair, exhausted.

Bertram Ruttle was happily playing his rib-bone xylophone to a group of young ghosts, who were dancing happily. Edith scowled at them.

'Bertram – I've never understood why you like playing music for those brats!' she shuddered. 'Children should be seen and not heard. And preferably not even seen! Those children in the school are even more dreadful than this lot! I have a feeling that those awful boys are on to me. I *have* to find a way of carrying out my plan, and quickly. Slow and painful just isn't going to work any more, however much fun it would have been.'

She poked a passing child ghost with her skinny finger.

'I need to take action immediately! What to do . . . what to do . . .?' She got up and started to pace backwards and forwards, kicking a passing rat. It squealed and scuttled into a pile of skulls for safety.

Bertram carried on playing. He nodded and shook his head as Edith spoke. He wasn't really listening.

'The problem is, Bertram, nobody even seems to have been poisoned yet, or even got sick. Either modern people are much tougher than I imagined, or those terrible school dinners have given them cast-iron stomachs. My plan is just not working quickly enough.'

She rummaged through her shelves again, picking up bottles and jars. 'Perhaps the ingredients I presumed were poisonous just aren't as bad as I thought.'

Her hand closed on a dusty old box hidden at the back of the shelf. She wiped off the cobwebs and popped them into her mouth. There was a black cat symbol on the box and a label saying 'Aggie Malkin's Hex Emporium'.

'Aggie!' she shouted. Two dozy bats flew off the top shelf, blinking with surprise. Edith dropped the box and ran off down a dingy tunnel. As the box hit the floor some red powder drifted out and landed on a passing spider. It blinked, stretched its eight legs and, in a puff of glittery smoke, had gone.

'Aggie! Aggie! I need your help!' yelled Edith, but all she could hear in the tunnel was her own voice echoing back at her.

She started to panic. She grabbed a passing ghost who was ferreting about in the sludge looking for beetles.

'Have you seen that witch, Aggie Malkin, anywhere?' demanded Edith. The ghost gazed at her blankly. Edith pushed him away.

'Ag-gie!' she called. 'I need you to cast a spell on tomorrow's school dinner – there's no time to waste!'

Then she heard a low, rumbling sound coming from a small side chamber, and she poked her head inside. A heap of black rags seemed to be inflating and deflating.

Strange . . . thought Edith. She prodded the heap with her foot.

'Wossat?' the heap snorted, erupting in a cloud of black velvet and rags as Aggie the ghost witch leaped to her feet.

'Who dares disturb my rest?' she bellowed. Her wand was drawn, and green sparks flew from the end. She pushed her hat back on her head. The pointed top flopped across her eyes.

'Aggie – it's me, Edith!'

'Might have known . . .' muttered Aggie. She put her wand away and leant on her broomstick.

'That's a beautiful fur collar you are wearing, Aggie – you *are* looking smart,' smarmed Edith.

'Firstly,' the witch sighed, 'flattery is not necessary. Tell me what you wish and I will help or not according to my desire. Secondly, take your hand off the "collar". It's Lilith Skitterpaws, my witch's cat and familiar.'

Edith froze. She may be dead, but Lilith Skitterpaws was vicious. She'd been known to bite chunks of ectoplasm off unsuspecting spectres and swallow it without chewing.

The cat hissed, and a threatening growl started in her throat. First one emerald eye glittered in the darkness, then two, and a pink mouth, bearing two rows of sharp, white teeth opened, then snapped shut. Edith jumped, but the cat was only yawning. It yowled, and she shot backwards.

'Pardon my familiar,' Aggie laughed.

'Familiar? I think she's downright rude!'
grumbled Edith.

The cat started to purr, and settled down for
another sleep.

'What do you want, Edith?' Aggie asked.

'Weeell, to see my old friend Aggie, of course!'
Edith smiled, exposing her brown, rotten teeth.

'Apart from that!' Aggie said, rolling her eyes.
Then she picked them up and put them back in
her eye sockets.

'I *would* appreciate a favour,' Edith wheedled.

'Go on then, what is it?' Aggie asked, starting
to light ghostly candles in alcoves around the
chamber. The flickering flames made her face
glow eerily. She pulled off her hat and fluffed
out her long black hair, clipping it back with
a small lizard that had been dozing on a clump
of wet fungus.

Edith stared at the floor, shuffling her feet.

'Go ahead, I'm all ears.'

Edith looked up and jumped. Aggie was
covered from head to toe in ears: rabbit ears,
fox ears, cat ears and bat ears!

'Just my little joke,' Aggie giggled, returning to
normal. 'Come on,' she said. 'What are you after?

I once turned a rather snooty lord's feast into horse poo. You should have seen his face! He had a mouthful at the time.'

'I want a spell to make the school dinners so poisonous that people drop dead as soon as the food touches their lips. Children, teachers – the whole lot! I want them all dead and St Sebastian's empty.'

Aggie stared at Edith in silence. 'But, Edith, that's dark magic. It's not my way. It's against my beliefs. That kind of dark magic brings terrible payback to the spell-caster. No, I won't do it!'

'Oh, please, Aggie, I'll make it worth your while . . .' Edith begged.

Aggie stared at a tall candle in front of her.

By the time Edith had finished nagging, the candle was just a tiny stub.

'Oh, all right, all right!' Aggie huffed. 'I'll meet you halfway. I'll give you a fast-acting ageing spell to make everyone get older quicker. That way, they'll grow too old for school and leave you alone.'

She pulled a piece of parchment from her *Book of Shadows* and began to write.

'Erm, Aggie . . . I can't read,' Edith whispered.

'Oh, for goodness' sake! You uneducated women make me furious! You'll have to listen carefully and learn the spell off by heart instead then,' she grumbled.

Edith clapped her hands together with glee and listened to Aggie's spell.

She was concentrating so hard that she didn't notice William hovering nearby, behind a pile of spell books. He nodded to himself and drifted off, back to the amphitheatre.

CHAPTER 11
PLAN-TASTIC

James, Lenny and Alexander were on their way
to school together the next morning. They'd
stayed up late on the phone to each another
the night before, and were still discussing the
Miss Grub situation as they walked.

'Well, she's clearly no TV chef,' James said.
'And if she *is* a ghost – which I think she must
be – she's bound to be up to no good.'

'I couldn't believe it when she started to stack
those sticks in the oven. I thought she'd gone
mad!' said Lenny, his eyes wide.

Alexander nodded. 'Well, the fact that she was trying to cook over a fire is consistent with the medieval period of history. Women spent hours collecting bundles of wood called *faggots* . . .'

'A little focus, professor? Not really the time for a history lesson, is it . . .?' said James, frowning.

Alexander smiled, sheepishly.

'What we need to do is to take action,' continued James. 'We need to sneak back into the kitchen at morning break and put a stop to her awful cookery before she serves up another gruesome meal – eh, Lenny?' he elbowed his friend in the ribs.

'I couldn't eat my breakfast this morning thinking about that eye looking at me yesterday . . .' Lenny shuddered. 'My mum nearly kept me off school because she thought I was coming down with something. I told her it was just something I'd eaten . . .' he retched suddenly. 'Can we change the subject?'

101

James punched Lenny on the shoulder. 'Sorry, Lenny! No can do. We need to make a plan. As I was saying, if we sneak across to the kitchen one by one during morning break . . .'

'You know, Lenny has a point,' groaned Alexander. 'My belly feels a bit weird too. Yesterday's foul stew I suppose. Perhaps it would be better if we didn't go over to the kitchen today . . .?'

'It's got to be today. No wimping out on me. We're in this together!' James said, firmly. 'Surely you don't want to chance the school getting closed down by the environmental health inspectors on account of its dodgy dinners, Stick? Imagine what that would do to your dad's reputation.'

Alexander looked sheepish. He knew when he was beaten.

'Worse than that, people could get hurt. Who knows what that ghost is adding to the food? It could get serious,' James added.

'Do you think we should tell my dad if there's something dangerous going on?' asked Alexander.

'Er, reality check!' James cried. 'Can you imagine the conversation? *Oh, well, Dad — it's like this: there's a ghost in the school who wants to shut it down and she's adding gross things to the dinner, like eyeballs and stuff.*' He changed his voice to imitate Mr Tick. '*Oh, is that right, son? Hang on while I call the loony bin and ask them to save you a bed.*'

Alexander's lip wobbled.

'I suppose it *does* sound a bit daft when you say it like that . . .' he mumbled.

'Cheer up! We'll be able to deal with this ourselves — you'll see,' James said. Alexander looked at his friend and smiled weakly. 'We'll go to the kitchens at morning break and see what we can do.'

Meanwhile, back in the sewer, someone else had hatched a plan. William had panicked when he heard Edith's awful scheme so, once he'd thought of an idea that just might scupper it, he'd dashed off to find Ambrose.

'We'll hide in the kitchen and Edith won't see us. When she tries to cast the spell, I'll add a line that'll reverse the spell. I think it'll work . . .'

'I hope so, son!' Ambrose smiled, as reassuringly as he could manage. 'I hope so.'

Far above the ghosts, the bell was ringing for morning break.

'Everyone ready for action?' James said to his friends.

Lenny and Alexander looked at each other and sighed heavily.

'Yes . . .' Lenny replied reluctantly, on behalf of both of them.

One at a time, the boys sneaked across the playground to the kitchen.

Mrs Meadows wandered backwards and forwards fetching pans and ingredients. Her eyes were glazed and her feet dragged across the floor as she walked.

105

'She looks like a zombie!' Alexander whispered. 'I suppose the ghosts have done some kind of mind meld with her to alter her perception . . .' Alexander's voice petered out as he saw James and Lenny scowling at him, unable to follow what he was talking about.

'We'll take turns to sneak in and hide,' said James. 'Each time Mrs Meadows opens the door, one of us can go in. You first, Lenny. You can choose the first place to hide because it'll have to be big!'

'Oh, ha flamin' ha!' Lenny groaned, holding his sides in mock hilarity.

'Hey, Lenny – don't hide in the fridge!' Alexander whispered.

'I wasn't going to – why?' Lenny replied.

'Well, they say you can tell an elephant's been in the fridge by the footprints in the butter. Imagine how easily they'd know you'd been in there, with your size tens!'

106

'What a comedian . . . *not!*' Lenny hissed, as he shot through the open door.

'Your turn next!' James said to Alexander. Alexander swallowed.

At that moment, Mrs Meadows opened the door again. As it swung shut, Alexander slipped through. James was left waiting alone. He could hear water running and cutlery being dropped, but no screaming or shouting. *They must be well hidden*, he thought.

The next time Mrs Meadows came out, he was ready. He slithered past her and rolled under a table. He banged into Alexander, and Lenny's face appeared behind him.

Nice to know we're all so original, thought James.

Back underground, William, with Ambrose following close behind, was on his way up the pipe from the sewer to the big kitchen sink.

Every now and again, dirty water gushed past the two ghosts. They could hear crashing and banging coming from the kitchen as Edith Codd, still posing as Miss Grub, carried out her evil plan. As they grew closer, they could hear strange chanting.

'She's started the spell!' cried William. 'I hope we're not too late!'

'Don't you worry, William,' Ambrose said, soothingly. If the young ghost had been able to turn round in the narrow pipe, he would have noticed that Ambrose's expression didn't match his reassuring words. He looked very worried indeed.

'OK – we're there. Time to get invisible!' William whispered.

The ghosts shimmered and winked out like a light. There was a sudden, gassy noise and a rat, pitter-pattering happily along what he thought was an empty pipe, fainted.

'Pardon me!' said Ambrose, as a waft of stinking gas wafted past William's face.

The ghosts slid out of the pipe and positioned themselves in the corner of the kitchen.

Miss Grub was hunched over a huge metal vat of thin, green gruel. She was muttering phrases and stopping, then starting again. She scratched her head and huge flakes of dandruff drifted into her cooking.

'I can't remember . . . Come along, Edith – think! You can do it!' she hissed to herself, battering her fist against the side of her head. 'Now, what did she say? . . .

Older now and older still,

Swallow now this bitter swill,

Consume the potion in your tum . . . Or was it bum? I can't remember!'

Lenny tittered despite himself.

Edith's head spun round. 'What was that? Oh, great – now I'm hearing things too . . .'

she muttered. She went back to trying to remember the spell.

James scowled at Lenny.

'Sorry! I'm nervous,' he whispered. 'When she said "bum" it made me laugh . . .' He gave an embarrassed shrug.

James shook his head.

'Come on, Edith, time's wasting . . .' the dinner lady muttered.

'Older now and older still,
Swallow now this bitter swill,
Consume the potion in your tum, and . . . and . . .'

William leant in close to Miss Grub's revolting ear and whispered, *'Grow much younger than your mum . . .'*

Without thinking, the dinner lady repeated the line after him.

At that moment, Mr Wharpley burst into the kitchen carrying a small bunch of daisies picked from the flowerbed outside the headmaster's office. *Nice-looking woman, that new dinner lady,* he'd thought. *I think I'll pay her a visit.*

Edith looked at Mr Wharpley through Miss Grub's eyes. *What now?* she wondered.

The caretaker marched across the kitchen and thrust the flowers into her hands.

Miss Grub looked at them, blankly. 'Is this posy of flowers a tussie-mussie? Are you a plague-carrier? What's going on here?' she muttered.

Mr Wharpley decided to taste the pot of soup. *It looks a bit thin, but I know women love it when you flatter their cooking,* he thought to himself.

James, Lenny and Alexander saw what was about to happen. As the caretaker raised the spoonful of bewitched soup to his lips, the boys sprang from under the table and charged towards him. Everything seemed to move in slow motion. James ran the fastest, with his arms outstretched, ready to knock the spoon out of Mr Wharpley's hand.

111

'Noooooo!' he roared. But it was too late. Mr Wharpley had already pushed the spoon of soup into his mouth, and had swallowed.

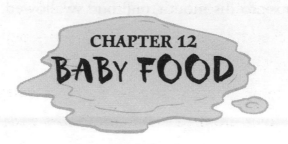

CHAPTER 12
BABY FOOD

The boys looked on in horror. As they stared
at Mr Wharpley, he began to change.

'I think he's getting younger!' James breathed
in amazement.

'Wow! It's like watching time-lapse
photography – you know, like the film sequences
where the seasons change and plants grow
before your very eyes . . .' Alexander said.

The caretaker's thin, grey hair thickened and
darkened. It coiled at the front of his head like
a thick, lazy snake.

'It's an Elvis quiff!' Lenny pointed.

The man's skin became smoother and his rather stained teeth started to grow whiter. He flicked his quiff back and winked saucily at Miss Grub.

She jumped, and started to try to re-cast the spell. James groaned and Lenny's eyes widened with horror.

'Mr Wharpley is . . . flirting! *Yuck!*' he whispered.

Miss Grub was muttering something and the boys looked over at her. She was waving her arms and chanting like a woman possessed.

Alexander glanced back at Mr Wharpley. 'He's getting even younger!' he shrieked.

The caretaker was now a spotty teenager, glaring moodily at the boys. Lenny and James spun round to look.

'He's only a few years older than us now – what's *happening*?' Lenny gasped.

'It must be some sort of tear in the space–time continuum!' Alexander cried.

'Never mind that science-fiction rubbish!' James shouted. 'What do we *do*?'

Miss Grub was now bellowing snippets of spell, horribly mangled, at the top of her voice. She flapped her arms in panic.

'*Older now and older still,*
Poke your eyeball with this . . . with this . . . quill?
Stir the potion with your thumb . . .'

She turned towards the boys, her eyes wild. 'Get away from me, you awful brats!' she shrieked. 'Why must you interfere with my plans?'

'Er, maybe because you're trying to poison our school dinners – *duh!*' James bellowed back at her.

Miss Grub looked at James with a face that was a mask of pure evil. Flames of madness flickered in her eyes. She ran to the sink and yelled down the plughole.

117

'Heeelp! Heeelp! Ambrose! William! Lady Grimes – *anybody*!'

She didn't realise Ambrose and William were there, watching everything from the corner of the kitchen. They watched as she picked up a small pan and scooped up some of the gruel.

'James! Alexander! Lenny!' William warned, but his voice was lost in all the shouting and mayhem.

Miss Grub began sloshing the bewitched gruel at the boys, including Mr Wharpley, who was now an eight-year-old with scabby knees and scruffy hair. His adult clothing hung from his shoulders, loosely.

'Quick! Grab a pan lid!' James shouted, throwing a lid to each of the boys. 'Use it like a shield!'

They whipped the lids in front of them as Miss Grub launched a barrage of splashes straight at them. By now, her eyes were glowing and she was foaming at the mouth.

'Get behind me, er . . . Mr Wharpley!' Lenny
shouted.

The caretaker was about four years old now,
and looked at Miss Grub with wide, frightened
eyes. He slid a dirty thumb towards his mouth.

At that moment, Ambrose and William took
action. They swooped on Miss Grub and hoisted
her off her feet.

119

The boys looked on in amazement as the dinner lady seemed to fly through the air and drop with a 'plop' into the vat of gruel.

With a strange fizzing sound she was gone.

CHAPTER 13
MAGIC STICK

A choking, green fog billowed out of the vat.

'Quick! Grab it!' James shouted. The boys,
unaware that the invisible William and Ambrose
were helping them, heaved the pan over to the
sink. 'Careful it doesn't slosh on you!'

They hurled the foul gruel down the drain.
A horrible gurgling, grinding sound filled the
kitchen.

'Yuck! It sounds just like my mum's waste-
disposal unit chewing up chicken bones,'
shuddered Lenny.

121

'Grab Mr Wharpley, quickly! We've got to smuggle him back into the main building without anyone seeing. He's going to disappear without a trace if we don't do something!' James shouted.

The caretaker was now a chubby toddler. He waved his arms and babbled baby talk as Lenny picked him up.

Wrapping him in his blazer, Lenny started for the door. The boys ran towards the main building, scuttling along close to the walls.

'Make for Mr Wharpley's room in the cellar!' whispered James, as they made it unseen into the main building.

The three boys charged for the door and James heaved it open. They leapt into the room and slammed it shut.

'What now? If we don't act fast, Mr Wharpley will be a newborn baby!' Lenny fretted.

'I think . . . I might be able to remember the spell . . . I was listening hard,' Alexander said. He closed his eyes and started to rub his temples as he thought. Suddenly, he straightened and stood up. His eyes snapped open.

'I've got it! Put Mr Wharpley over here where I can see him.'

The caretaker giggled as Alexander waved his hands over his head. The boy began to chant:

123

'*Older now and older still,*
You've swallowed now the bitter swill,
Consumed the potion in your tum,
Become the same age as my mum.'

Mr Wharpley began to grow older. His bones seemed to liquefy and he grew taller. Alexander carried on chanting:

'*Return to where you were before,*
Once more a man stands on this floor!'

As Alexander finished with a flourish, Mr Wharpley was standing in front of them again. But it was a new, improved Mr Wharpley.

His hair was thicker and darker than before. He stood up straighter and had fewer wrinkles. James and Lenny raised their eyebrows at Alexander.

'It was the least I could do – make him a few years younger – after all he's been through . . .' Alexander said with a shrug.

At that moment, the caretaker's glazed eyes cleared and snapped into focus.

124

'What are you brats doing in here? You know my room's out of bounds to pupils! I would have thought you would have known better, Alexander! There are dangerous chemicals in here! And, more importantly, this is where I come to get away from you lot! Now go on – get lost! Go and make your mischief somewhere else!' He shooed them out of the door.

'*Charming!*' laughed Alexander, as he stumbled up the stairs.

'Same old Mr Wharpley!' James grinned. 'Thanks to you, Stick!'

'Yeah, nice one!' smiled Lenny. 'Business as usual – football, anyone?' The friends ran off on to the field.

Back in his sanctuary, Mr Wharpley hummed a happy little ditty as he watched the kettle came to the boil. He'd already forgotten his little adventure. He did an Elvis sneer and wiggled his hips as he hummed.

As the kettle started to whistle, he cracked open a packet of ginger creams. *I think I deserve a little treat,* he thought to himself, as he popped a biscuit into his mouth and crunched.

He caught sight of his reflection in the shiny kettle. *Lookin' good, Reggie boy!* he thought, as he smiled at himself.

The noise of Mr Wharpley's kettle boiling muffled the sounds of Edith's frustrated screams coming from the sewers below.

She was pacing up and down in a fury.

'I just don't understand it!' she shrieked, tugging at her wispy hair with rage. 'Why didn't my plan work? It was brilliant!'

She glared at Ambrose, who was stifling a giggle. At the last moment, he turned it into a hacking cough, and blew a chunk of green slime on to the wall. It slithered down and plopped on to the head of a sleeping rat, giving it a green-jelly wig.

'The thing that's really puzzling me is how those scrawny little boys managed to heave the vat of soup across to the sink . . .' Edith mused. 'I mean, I understand how they managed to get slender little *me* into the pan.' She stroked her hands over her scrawny hips, and Ambrose shuddered. 'But that pan was *heavy*!'

William disguised a smirk.

'Well, Edith, it must have been because they were really, really scared of you. You know, like their fear gave them extra reserves of strength or something . . .'

Ambrose spluttered again, and William couldn't help joining in.

'Oh, shut up and get out of my sight, you stupid ghosts!' Edith snapped.

Ambrose and William hurried off down a tunnel. Edith heard the sound of distant laughter.

'I don't know what they've got to be so happy about!' Edith scowled to herself.

She flounced across to a bench made from tatty old bones and sat down, rubbing her temples. Flakes of skin fluttered down, collecting in her lap.

Suddenly, she sat up straight. 'Pull yourself together, Edith!' she muttered to herself. 'One day, St Sebastian's, I *will* find a way to close you down – and victory will be mine!' she hissed through gritted teeth.

Two bats, disturbed by her grumbling, fluttered around the amphitheatre. They chattered, and it sounded like laughter.

'And you can shut up, too!' Edith roared, hurling a handful of knucklebones in their direction.

SURNAME: Harbottle

FIRST NAME: Ambrose

AGE: 612

HEIGHT: 1.75 metres

EYES: Hollow and dark, with heavy bags underneath them

HAIR: Has been thin on top since 1341

FACT FILE

LIKES: Leeches — he used to sell them before the Black Death carried him off (he's still partial to the odd one as a snack). Also taking naps, putting his feet up and staying out of Edith's schemes

DISLIKES: Too much hard work; anywhere clean and tidy; sweet smells

SPECIAL SKILL: Can work out the age of a leech just by tasting it

INTERESTING FACT: Ambrose actually quite enjoys life in the St Sebastian's sewer system. When he was alive, his house was a dark, dingy hovel and the stinking sewer reminds him of home!

For more facts on Ambrose Harbottle, go to **www.too-ghoul.com**

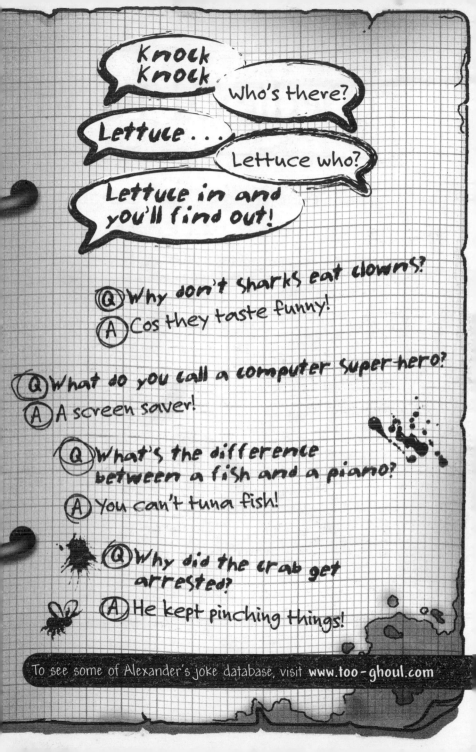

Medieval Food

And you thought your school dinners were bad. Check out what people ate in medieval times!

There were no fridges so fish, meat and fruit were pickled to stop them going mouldy.

At banquets, it was common to have a whole roast pig – head and all – in the middle of the table.

'**F**estooned boar's head' was another delicacy served for the king. Yuck!

Having a roast fowl was common at feasts – but the cook would put the feathers and head back on the bird after it was cooked to make it look alive!

The Facts!

Sailors at sea often ran out of food and had to eat leather, rats and maggots to survive.

Fast food was already invented: people bought cooked birds like larks to nibble on when they needed a quick snack!

A popular medieval drink was the rather yucky-sounding 'chicken beer'. It must have been fowl! (Geddit?)

In those days, people didn't waste any part of an animal, so there were lots of recipes for pigs trotters, chicken feet and gross bits like brains and stomachs.

Groo!

Ye Olde Plague Pitte Restaurante

DINNER MENU

By ~~Miss Grubb~~
Edith

STARTERS
Oozing coffin-
slime soup
Flaky skin salad
Fresh leeches*

MAIN COURSES
Worm bolognese
Roast rat with all
the trimmings
Bone surprise

DESSERTS
Sewage mousse
Crunchy
beetle cake
I scream

Service by a gruesome skeleton not included. And no
moaning or we'll send you up to the St Sebastian's canteen
for lunch. Then you'll know what gross grub is!

*Farmed by Ambrose

Can't wait for the next book in the series?
Here's a sneak preview of

ATTACK OF THE ZOMBIE NITS!

available now from all good bookshops,
or **www.too-ghoul.com**

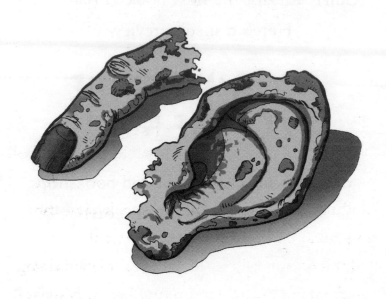

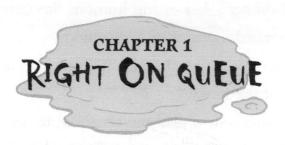

CHAPTER 1
RIGHT ON QUEUE

'Where's the best place for a sickroom at school?' asked Alexander Tick in the lunchtime queue. Without pausing for a reply, he delivered the punchline: 'Right next to the canteen!'

Pupils around him groaned and turned away. His friends, James Simpson and Lenny Maxwell, shared a glance.

'It's bad enough that we have to queue up for twenty minutes every day,' moaned James. 'Don't feel you have to entertain us as well.'

137

'Oh, it's no problem!' beamed Alexander, missing James's point entirely. 'I've got dozens of school-dinner jokes in my humour database, and I memorised them all this morning.'

A cry of despair echoed out along the lunch queue at the news.

'Did you hear about the cruel dinner lady?' he asked, glancing up and down the line for a willing victim to aim the rest of the joke at. 'She beat the eggs and whipped the cream!'

Lenny sighed. 'If it wasn't for the fact that my stomach thinks my mouth's on strike, I'd be racing in terror across the sports field right now,' he said.

'If you decide to head out that way, do us all a favour and take Stick with you,' said James. 'You could bury him in the sand pit at the long jump.'

'Oh, here's a good one . . .' began Alexander. Once again, the queue let out a collective moan. James spun round and glared at him.

138

'You're not winning us any friends here, you know,' he hissed.

Alexander shrugged. 'Who needs friends when you've got an audience?' James shook his head and turned away. 'What kind of food do maths teachers eat?' continued Alexander.

Suddenly, the very large and very angry figure of Gordon 'The Gorilla' Carver forced his way back through the queue and grabbed Alexander's collar, shoving him hard against the wall. 'You finish that joke and I'll push your teeth so far down your throat you'll have to sit on your chips to chew them!' he threatened.

'G-Gordon!' stammered Alexander. 'You're not a comedy fan then?'

The Gorilla scratched his head and snarled. 'Oh, I like comedy,' he spat. 'I just don't like the rubbish you spout!'

'Well, it is a very s–subjective medium,' smiled Alexander as the bully pressed him harder

against the wall. 'Th-the word "subjective"
means some people like it, and others don't,'
he explained.

James turned away, unable to watch. 'Does he actually *want* to spend the rest of term in hospital?' he asked Lenny.

'Why, thank you,' leered Gordon sarcastically, scratching at his scalp again and pressing his face into Alexander's. 'The question is, do you know what the word "pain" means?'

'Well, the dictionary describes "pain" as –' began the reply.

'*Alexander!*' yelled James and Lenny together.

'Oh,' said their friend, realising that he was just seconds away from yet another beating at the hands of The Gorilla.

'Look, Carver,' said James, stepping into the bully's line of sight. 'I'll make sure he doesn't tell any more jokes. Just let him go and I'll buy you an extra dessert, OK?'

Gordon's eyes drifted out of focus briefly as he considered the offer then, with a grunt, he released Alexander's collar and began to push his way back to his place at the head of the queue, scratching at his head once more.

James spun round to face Alexander. '*Now* will you keep quiet?' he demanded. 'Not only have you just cost me the price of a rhubarb crumble, you've even managed to annoy Gordon's nits!'

The entire canteen fell silent as Gordon stopped, mid-scratch, and slowly turned around. 'What did you say?' he roared.

James became aware that other pupils were stepping away from him, clearing a path for The Gorilla to advance. 'I-I didn't . . .' he stuttered.

Gordon lurched forwards, grabbing a scoop of ice cream from a bowl on a nearby table and hurling it at James. The dessert's original owner opened her mouth to complain, then saw the Gorilla's face and thought better of it.

The ice cream landed with a 'splat' on James's shoulder, and the lunch queue erupted in laughter; laughter which stopped short when a blob of custard hit Gordon square in the face. Everyone turned to see Lenny looking sheepish.

'What did you do that for?' whispered James.

'Seemed like a good idea at the time,' Lenny replied.

With a howl, Gordon raced forwards, snatching a handful of mashed potato from the plate of a year-nine girl. He jumped on Lenny, rubbing it into the boy's face. Alexander and James leapt into action, pulling food from other tables and hurling it at the back of Gordon's head.

Within seconds, the entire canteen had erupted into a massive food fight. Cold chips, blackened sausages and tasteless peas flew everywhere as the pupils finally had the courage to treat the school menu with the respect it deserved.

The door to the kitchen burst open, and two dinner ladies raced out, ducking to avoid being covered with lumpy gravy.

'Stop this *right now*!' roared Mrs Cooper.

143

'We *slaved* over this food!' bellowed Mrs Meadows.

At this, the attack switched to the original source of the foul food – the dinner ladies. The two women scuttled across the canteen, hands over their heads, as they were pelted with soggy vegetables and slices of tough beef.

Reaching the centre of the battle, the dinner ladies pulled Lenny and Gordon apart.

'You're going straight to the headmaster's office!' shouted Mrs Cooper, as a glob of custard hit the back of her neck.

'You two as well!' added Mrs Meadows, grabbing James and Alexander before they could hurry away.

'What have *I* done?' moaned Alexander.

Mrs Meadows spat out a mouthful of limp carrot. 'We have to stand behind that counter every day listening to your so-called jokes!' she cried. 'It's payback time!'

Braving a fresh rain of school food, the two dinner ladies dragged the boys towards the canteen doors. As he was marched away, Alexander wiped cold gravy from his eyes and smiled.

'You know, this reminds me of the teacher who ordered a different school dinner every day of the year . . .' he began.

James pulled a handful of mashed turnip from his hair and forced it into Alexander's mouth, silencing him.

'I knew this stuff was good for something,' he muttered.